PENROD AGAIN

by Mary Blount Christian

illustrated by Jane Dyer

Penrod Porcupine and Griswold Bear are back! In this companion book to PENROD'S PANTS, Penrod is still causing trouble for his friend, Griswold. Whether it's picture-taking, spring cleaning, moving, or housework, Penrod's schemes create havoc for the good-natured bear. Yet in the last of their five encounters, Penrod plans an early Christmas celebration that proves to be just right.

PENROD AGAIN

Mary Blount Christian

Pictures by Jane Dyer

Ready-to-Read

Macmillan Publishing Company
New York

Collier Macmillan Publishers
London

To Carol Farley
—M.B.C.

For Emily and Jacob,
who are moving far away
—J.D.

Text copyright © 1987 by Mary Blount Christian
Illustrations copyright © 1987 by Jane Dyer
All rights reserved. No part of this book may be reproduced or transmitted
in any form or by any means, electronic or mechanical, including photocopying,
recording or by any information storage and retrieval system,
without permission in writing from the Publisher.
Macmillan Publishing Company
866 Third Avenue, New York, NY 10022
Collier Macmillan Canada, Inc.
Printed and bound by South China Printing Company, Hong Kong
First American Edition

10 9 8 7 6 5 4 3 2 1

The text of this book is set in 18 pt. Century Expanded.
The illustrations are rendered in pencil and watercolor.

Library of Congress Cataloging-in-Publication Data
Christian, Mary Blount.
Penrod again.
(Ready-to-read)
Summary: The adventures of two friends who sometimes
argue, but really love and support each other.
[1. Porcupines—Fiction. 2. Bears—Fiction.
3. Friendship—Fiction] I. Dyer, Jane, ill.
II. Title. III. Series.
PZ7.C4528Pd 1987 [E] 86-21846
ISBN 0-02-718550-8

CONTENTS

SPRING FEVER

Penrod Porcupine
had his mop.
He had his broom.
He had rags
and a bucket.
"Get up!"
he told Griswold Bear.
"It is time
for spring cleaning.
I will help you.
Then you can help me."

Griswold sat up in bed.

"Spring already?"

he asked.

He yawned.

"I do not want

to do spring cleaning.

I have spring fever."

"Fever?"
Penrod said.
"That sounds serious.
You should stay in bed."

"Hmmm," Griswold said.
"You are right, Penrod.
I should stay in bed."

"Do not worry," Penrod said.

"I will clean your house.

I will cook for you

until you are well again.

I will have you up

in no time."

Griswold crawled

under the covers.

"You are a true friend,"

he said.

He closed his eyes.

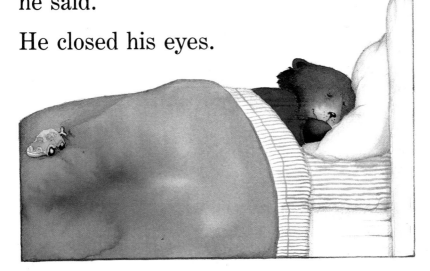

Mmmmmmmmmmm.

Griswold sat up in bed.
He grunted.
"What is that?" he asked.

Mmmmmmmmmmm.

"Go to sleep," Penrod said.
"I am vacuuming."

"Why in here?"
Griswold moaned.

Mmmmmmmmmmm. Thup!

Griswold sat up again.
"And what was *that?*"

"Do not worry," Penrod said.

"Your vacuum cleaner ate a tie.
That is all."

Griswold's lip turned down.
"The one with the palm tree?"

9

Penrod opened
the vacuum cleaner.
"See?" he said.
"The tie is okay.
You will just have to wear it
on the other side."

"*Grrrrr!*" Griswold growled.

"You sound worse!"
Penrod said.
"But do not worry.
I will cook some soup for you.
It is a sure cure for fever."

Griswold licked his lips.

"You are a true friend,"

he said.

He fluffed his pillow.

He closed his eyes.

He slept.

Clatter, clatter, crash!

Griswold sat up.

"What was that?" he asked.

"My fingers slipped,"
Penrod said.
"But do not worry.
It was only
an old blue cup."

Griswold pulled the covers
over his head.
"My *favorite* cup," he said.

"Go to sleep," Penrod said.
"I will take care of you.
I will have you up
in no time."

Griswold yawned.

He closed his eyes.

He slept.

"Griswold," Penrod said.

Griswold's eyes popped open.

"Do you have a soup pot?"

"In the cabinet!"
  Griswold said.

"Which cabinet?"
  Penrod asked.

"The *only* cabinet I have,"
  Griswold said.

"Which side of the cabinet?"
  Penrod asked.

"The *inside!*" Griswold said.

"You are so grumpy
   when you have a fever,"
   Penrod said.
"Go to sleep.
   I will have you up
   in no time."

Griswold sighed.
   He closed his eyes.
   He slept.

"Griswold," Penrod said.
   Griswold opened his eyes.
"I need a knife
   to cut the carrots."

"No, no!" Griswold said.
"I will do it!"

Griswold got out of bed.
"Penrod vacuumed up
my favorite tie."
He put on his T-shirt
and jeans.
"Penrod broke
my favorite cup."
He put on his socks
and sneakers.
"Penrod did not
let me sleep
for one minute."

16

"Penrod," Griswold said.
"I am ready
 for spring cleaning.
 I will help you
 clean your house.
 But please do not help me
 anymore."

"Griswold!" Penrod said.
"You are over your fever!
 I told you
 I would have you up
 in no time."

"*Grrrrr!*" Griswold said.

THE CAMERA

Penrod hurried next door
to Griswold's house.

"I have a camera,"
Penrod told Griswold.
"I cannot wait
to try it out."

"Why wait?" Griswold asked.
"I will take your picture.
Then you can take mine."

"That is a great idea,"
Penrod said.
"I will hang your picture
on my living room wall."

"And I will put your picture
on my mantel," Griswold said.

"Let us go outside,"
Penrod said.

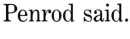

"What kind of picture
do you want?"
Griswold asked.

"I want a brave picture,"
Penrod said.
He climbed onto the fence.
He held his arms out straight.
He stood on one foot.
Penrod smiled.

Click!

"Oh, what a good picture!"
Griswold said.
"You looked very brave.
Now take mine."

Griswold gave the camera
to Penrod.
He climbed onto the fence.
He held his arms out straight.
The fence wiggled.
He stood on one foot.
The fence wobbled.
Griswold's arms flapped.

"That is very good!"
Penrod said.
"Why don't you smile?
Then I can take your picture."

Crash!
Griswold fell.
Click!
Penrod snapped the picture.

"*Grrrrr!*" Griswold said.
He rubbed his knee.
"I do not want
a *falling* picture,"
he said.

"Next time I will not wait
for a smile,"
Penrod promised.

"And I do not want
a *brave* picture.
I want a *nice, natural* picture."

"Okay," Penrod said.
"Stand by the fish pond.
I will take your picture again."

j39291

Griswold stood by the pond.
"I will keep both feet
on the ground,"
he said.
"And I will smile *now*."
Griswold grinned.

Penrod looked
through the camera.
"You look fuzzy.
Back up a little."

Griswold backed up.
He did not stop smiling.

"Back up more," Penrod said.
"You still look fuzzy!"

Griswold backed up some more.
Click!
Penrod snapped the picture.
Splash!
Griswold fell into the pond.

"*Grrrrr!*" Griswold growled.
"I do not want
a *wet* picture, either."

Griswold crawled
out of the pond.
He shook himself off.

"Do not worry,"
Penrod said.
"I took the picture
before you fell in.
It will be a nice, natural,
feet-on-the-ground picture."

Griswold pulled a fish
from his pocket.
He threw it back
into the pond.

"I cannot wait
to see the pictures,"
Griswold said.
"Let me change
into some dry clothes.
Then we can take the film
to the store."

Penrod looked puzzled.
"Film?" he asked.
"Nobody told me
I needed film!"

"*Grrrrr!*" Griswold said.

MOVING

Tap, tap, tap.

Penrod put up a sign
in his front yard.
It said FOR SALE.

"You are moving!"
Griswold said.
"This is awful!"

"It is?" Penrod asked.
"The new house is much nicer."

"But I will miss you,
   dear friend Penrod,"
   Griswold said.

"You will?" Penrod asked.
"You are always growling at me.
   I thought you would not miss me,
   even if I moved far, far away."

"Oh, dear!" Griswold said.
"Far, far away?"

A moving van pulled up.
It belonged to Hugo
and Bruno Hippo.
They went into Penrod's house.
Penrod and Griswold followed.

"I am losing my dear,
dear friend,"
Griswold said.
He sniffled.
"Take my lucky clover.
Think of me sometime."

"Oh, dear!" Penrod said.

"You are such a good friend."

He packed the lucky clover.

"I will always think of you.

No matter where I am,

you will always be my friend."

Griswold snuffled.

"Boo hoo hoooo!

I may never see you again,"

he said.

"Take my ballpoint pen.

Carry it and remember me.

I will miss you

when you are far, far away."

Penrod put the ballpoint pen
in his pocket.
"How could I forget you?"
Penrod said.

"Boo hoo hoooooo!
Do you really have to move
so far, far away?"
Griswold asked.
He blew his nose.
"I will miss you so much."

Griswold gave Penrod
his flashlight.

"Use this when it is dark,"
he said.
"Use it and think of me."

"I will, I will!"
Penrod said.

"And take my red umbrella.
When it rains, open it.
Remember that Griswold
likes you very much."

Penrod dried his eyes.
"I will, dear friend Griswold.
Write to me," he said.
He crawled into the truck
with the Hippo brothers.
Penrod waved good-bye.

Griswold waved back.

He watched the truck disappear
around the corner.

"I may never see my dear
friend again," he said.

Griswold sighed.

He went into his backyard.

He sat down on his steps.

He thought about his friend.

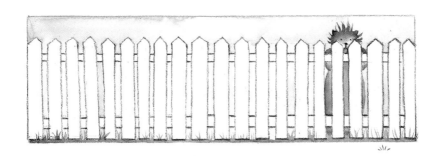

Suddenly,
two eyes peeked at him
over the back fence.
"Penrod!" Griswold said.
"Is that really you?"

Penrod smiled and waved.

"I gave you my lucky clover.
I gave you my ballpoint pen,"
Griswold said.
"I gave you my flashlight.
I gave you my red umbrella
because you were moving!"

"I *did* move," Penrod said.

"But I thought you were moving
  far, far away," Griswold said.

"To tell you the truth,"
  Penrod said,
"I was so sad that I forgot
  I would be living
  right behind you."

"*Grrrrr!*" Griswold said.

TOO SMALL

"My house is too small,"
  Griswold said.
"I need more space."

"My new house is dingy,"
  Penrod said.
"It needs painting.
  Help me paint.
  I will help you
  build a new room."

Penrod got paint.

He got brushes and rollers.

"Some of my furniture
is in the way," he said.

"We must put it
someplace else."

Griswold frowned.
"Where?"

"At your house,"
Penrod said.

"Why my house?"
Griswold asked.
"It is too small."

"Do not worry.

We will paint quickly.

Then my furniture

can come right back."

They put Penrod's reading chair

in Griswold's kitchen.

They put Penrod's lamp

in Griswold's hall.

They put Penrod's table and chairs

in Griswold's living room.

"Too small," Griswold said.

"Too crowded."

They went back to Penrod's.
All day they painted.
At last they finished.

"Let us put everything back,"
    Griswold said.

"But the paint is still wet,"
    Penrod said.
"We must wait until tomorrow."

"I am going home,"
    Griswold said.
"I will read a book.
    Then I will go to sleep."

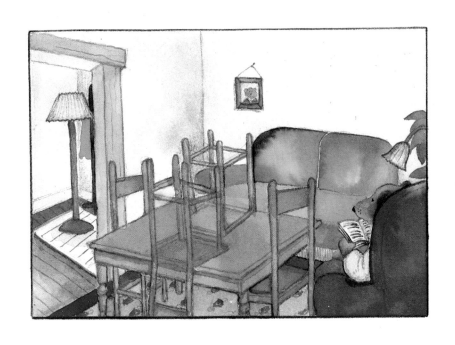

Griswold went home.
He squeezed
past Penrod's lamp.
He crawled
over Penrod's table.
He sat down
in his reading chair.

Knock, knock.

There was someone
at the door.
Griswold crawled
over Penrod's table.

He squeezed
past Penrod's lamp.
He opened the door.

It was Penrod.
"Now what?" Griswold asked.

"The paint smells terrible,"
Penrod said.
"I will have to sleep
on your couch."

They squeezed
past Penrod's lamp.
They climbed
over Penrod's table.
Penrod lay down
on the couch.
Griswold sat down
in his reading chair.
He picked up his book.

"I cannot sleep
with the light on,"
Penrod said.

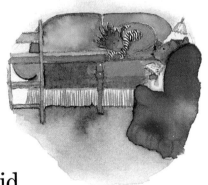

"*Grrrrr!*" Griswold said.
"My house is even smaller
than before."

"Do not worry," Penrod said.
"The paint will be dry
tomorrow.
We will put my things back.
Then I will help you
build a room.
Your house will be just right."

Griswold put down his book.
He crawled back
over Penrod's table.
In the kitchen,
he climbed over Penrod's chair
to get a drink of water.
Then he went to bed.

"Good-night!" Penrod called.

"Good-night!" Griswold called.
"Grrrrr!" he said.

The next morning,
they carried Penrod's things
back to his house.

"Now I will help *you*,"
Penrod said.

They went to Griswold's.
Griswold walked straight
to his chair.
He sat down.
He stretched his legs.
"Ahhhhhh," Griswold said.

"Don't you want
to build a new room?"
Penrod asked.

Griswold leaned back.
He smiled.
"To tell you the truth,
now that your things are gone
my house is just right."

HOLIDAYS

"The Hippo brothers
have new jogging suits,"
Griswold said.

"They got them
for Christmas,"
Penrod said.
"Hyatt Giraffe says
it comes every winter,
while we are sleeping."

"It is not fair,"
Griswold said.
"I like presents, too."

"We are awake now,"
Penrod said.

"Let us have Christmas."

"How will we do that?"
Griswold asked.

"Do not worry,"
Penrod said.

"I know all about it.
There is snow—"

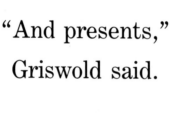

"And presents,"
Griswold said.

"And a Christmas tree,"
  Penrod said.

"And presents,"
  Griswold said.

  Penrod brought the tree
  from the woods.
"We will string berries,"
  he said.
"We will hang them
  on the tree."

"This is silly,"
Griswold grumbled.
"First we put
an outside tree inside.
Now we hang things
from other trees on it."

"Let us go to town
to buy the presents,"
Penrod said.

"What should I get you?"
Griswold asked.

"That is easy,"
Penrod said.
"Give me something
that *you* like.
That way you will know
it is a good gift."

"Okay," Griswold said.

Griswold went into one store.
Penrod went into another.
They met later.

Griswold shoved a bag
at Penrod.
"Here are your presents.
Where are mine?"

"First we must wrap them,"
  Penrod said.

"Why?" Griswold asked.

"So we can unwrap them,"
  Penrod said.

"*Grrrrr!*" Griswold said.
"But they *are* unwrapped.
  Why do we wrap them
  so we can unwrap them?"

Penrod took his presents home.
He wrapped them in red paper.
He tied them with white ribbon.
He took them to Griswold's.

Penrod and Griswold
put their presents
under the tree.
Together they baked
gingerbread cookies.
They made peppermint tea.

They sat by the tree
and ate cookies
and drank tea.
"It is time to open
our presents,"
Penrod said.

Penrod opened
one of his presents.
It was a jar of honey.

"I gave you honey
  because I love honey,"
  Griswold said.

"Thank you," Penrod said.

Griswold opened
one of his presents.
It was an ant farm.

"I love ants,"
  Penrod said.

"Thank you, Penrod,"
  Griswold said.
  He swallowed a *grrrrr.*

Penrod gave Griswold red mittens.

They were too small.

Griswold gave Penrod red mittens.

They were too big.

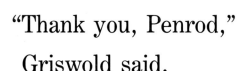

They traded presents.

"Thank you, Penrod,"
Griswold said.

"I just love my presents."

"My presents are perfect, too,"
Penrod said.

"Let us have Christmas again,"
  Griswold said.
"Only next time
  let us invite everyone."

"That is a good idea,"
  Penrod said.
"It will be even more fun."

"And we will have
  more presents,"
  Griswold said.

"Merry Christmas,"
  Penrod said.

"Merry Christmas,"
  Griswold said.